# Can You Read Me Now?
## The Story of a "Just Right" Book and His Dream of Being Discovered

Written and Illustrated
by Helga Henn

"To have a successful independent reading experience,
students need to know how to select a book.
Books can be easy, just right, or challenging for readers.
Readers need books that are just right."
*Richard Allington*

WIT Publishing for Education
Text and Illustrations Copyright © 2015 by Helga Henn

Printed in China

This book is dedicated to...

Mama, your beautiful heart and creative mind inspire mine every day.
You are always with me.

Papa, your standard of excellence and hard work are evidence that it can be done if you try.
I tried my best, just like you.

This book is also dedicated to each of my students... past, present and future.
Thank you for letting me see your best "you".
Because of you, I teach... and love it!
Thank you!

L.C., my dear friend, your wisdom and genuine support fill my heart with gratitude.

M.H. for sharing your creativity with me – Bobo and I thank you.

M.A. for bridging dreams and making them real.  You are an inspiration.

Special thanks to Aramoun Publishing for Education for all the
support and encouragement throughout this "first" project.

# Follow this story to learn...
## How to Choose a "Just Right" Book

- Look at the cover.

- Read the title and the name of the author.

- Read the summary of the book.

- Flip through the pages.

- Look at the pictures and words.

- Read the first 1-2 pages.

- Use the 5-Finger Rule to count challenging words on a page:

  0-1 fingers — too easy
  2-3 fingers — just right
  5 fingers — too hard

"You can't learn from a book you can't read."
*Richard Allington*

I am a book.

My life as a book can sometimes be very lonely.  That happens when I am too easy or too hard for people who want to read me, but can't.

I remember dreaming of the day when someone would discover me as a "just right" book.  I imagined they would be able to read all of me... once or even many times.  When that happened, I felt so loved.

I am a book.
I am the perfect book...
for somebody.

This is the story of how, one day, my dream came true.

One day I was resting on the library bookshelf feeling lonely and bored.

Children were passing me by and I didn't know why.

Did they think I was too hard or too easy?

Did they know what it meant to be a just right book?

I had to know more.  I patiently watched and waited

as children chose other books to read.

It wasn't long before a boy came by and stopped right in front of my bookshelf. "Could this be my chance?", I wondered.

I was feeling hopeful that he might see me and just then it happened... the boy glanced at all of us in the row, suddenly seeming to notice just me.

I was so excited!

He gently removed me from the bookshelf and handled me with care like a responsible reader would.

The boy looked at me with wonder and interest.  He began reading the title on my front cover.

Did he understand what my title meant?

After viewing my title, the boy read the name of the author, that person who held the pen that wrote my story.

That was a good start.

Then he rested me on his lap and quietly thought about what he saw.

It seemed that the boy wanted to know more about me.

I hoped he would keep looking... and he did.

If the boy could figure out that I was "just right" for him,

maybe he would try to read all of me.

He took his time thinking.

He quickly turned me over and read the words on my back cover.

The boy knew that reading every detail would help him make the right book choice.

He even knew that words on my back cover are the summary.

The summary is a good place to find out what my story is about before reading all of me.

The boy continued to look me over.   He flipped through my pages, looking to see what I was like... flipping quickly in some parts and pausing to turn the pages slowly in other places where he found me even more interesting.    I was really beginning to feel special.

As he looked through my pages,
the boy seemed to be searching for something, but what?

Right then I heard him say, "These pictures are so cool!"

The boy couldn't take his eyes off me.

He seemed relieved to find a book like me, even if I wasn't like those

BIG, popular books that other kids were carrying around.


The boy knew that pretend reading would not help.


He had tried that before, just to fit in with a group.

I saw it first hand from the comfort of my own shelf.

Some kids chose the BIG books to look cool but missed out on the fun

of reading books they could read well.


This time the boy found ME and was more comfortable than before.

The look on the boy's face told me I might be right for him. He began to whisper-read, then listened and said,

"Hey, some words are easy and just a few are hard. I think I want to try this book."

He read the first 1-2 pages and liked what he read... maybe it reminded him of something he had done before.

I loved what I was seeing.

This time it was me who couldn't take my eyes off of the boy.

Moments later he re-read my first page and began counting with his fingers.  I realized he was counting how many challenging words were on the first page.  He found two.

The boy remembered that strong readers use the 5-Finger Rule and knew to expect 2-3 challenging words on a page in a "just right" book.

I was a good choice!  The boy would finally know how it feels to read a book for a long time and might love me even more.

ear Young Readers,

at was a great day for the boy and for me, too.  Knowing I was the "just right" book made us both feel special. e next time you visit the library, look for me and I'll be there for you, too.

ntil that happens, take time to notice some things about yourself as a reader.  Think about the boy when you member what a strong reader does.  For example, use what you already know to make connections to a book at is new to you.  That will help you understand.  Listen to what you are reading… Does it sound right?  Does it ake sense?  Don't be afraid to go back and re-read.  That is always a good idea.

hen you were a very young reader, the right book for you may have been a picture book that you read so ten that you had it memorized… it was your favorite.  Someone read the words to you, together with you, and on you read by yourself.  That will happen again as you continue to learn and grow as a reader.

d you know that the types of "just right" books you choose will change as your reading improves?  It's true. ve new books a chance by finding a quiet place where you can think and build stamina while reading. member that strong readers use this and many more strategies to help themselves understand a story better.

hen you do what you've learned, other children who see you being responsible will want to be just like you.  Tell m about me so they can love reading like you do.

Your friend,

The "Just Right" Book

# Quick Check

## THIS BOOK IS TOO EASY IF:

*You have read the book many times before.
*Your thinking comes easily as you read.
*You can read it smoothly and in a snap.
*There are no challenging words.
*You know all the words in the book.

## THIS BOOK IS JUST RIGHT IF:

*The book looks interesting.
*You can figure out most words in the book.
*An adult has read this book aloud to you.
*You have read other books by this author.
*You know something about the subject

## THIS BOOK IS TOO CHALLENGING IF:

*There are too many words you can't figure out.
*It takes a long time to read one page.
*Many parts of the book are confusing.
*You don't know much about the topic.
*It is too difficult to enjoy.